Poetry From The Coal

Julia Scanlon

ISBN: 9781980556800
ISBN-13:

DEDICATION

Keep your hat tied tight little Welsh girl,
Keep your chin upright and look on high
That is our hill yonder, little Welsh girl,
That is trying so hard to touch the sky.
We are far from home, little Welsh girl,
But our hearts are buried on that hill.
It may seem so far away little Welsh girl-
But our souls stay Welsh and always will

For Joe Marenghi who like me is far from home. May we meet up again there some day...

And to my other Jo, I hope somewhere you are reading this and looking down on me. Never forgotten

CONTENTS

ACKNOWLEDGMENTS

To my Mam and Dad, who encouraged me to read and write from an early age, thank you for everything, and especially for my encyclopaedias- I know you had very little money and it must have been so hard for you to buy them but I treasured them, and am grateful for every other thing you did for me.

To all my friends, new and old, who have appreciated my little rhymes over the years, you have given me the confidence to have a try at writing. You are too many to name, but I appreciate each one of you.

To my children and my husband, who, despite being English, are all ok really! I love you more than anything in the world.

And a special mention to Pam Portlock- Pam, if nothing else comes of this book I have found a friend through its creation. Thank you for taking the time to read my rhymes and to feedback and thank you for believing in me when I don't even believe in myself. You are truly a gift.

Julia Scanlon

Introduction

Having grown up in the Rhondda Fach, in a little village called Ynyshir, I took for granted the community spirit that resided within it. It was in the sixties, and I had the freedom to move about as a child that my own children will never have.

I played on railway lines, I went to the park, I visited my family and went on outings with the local chapel. Neighbours came into my house as the door was always unlocked and all the grown-ups were called "Aunty' or "Uncle".

As I grow older and having moved to the other side of the world, I am quickly realising that I had so much in the palm of my hand but that I never appreciated it at the time.

In these days of social media, I have been able to take a trip down memory lane with friends from my younger days and this has fed my imagination. I am no Poet Laureate but enjoy penning rhymes for friends and family and thought this would be my way of revisiting my youth. I hope you enjoy this little collection.

Diolch Yn Fawr,

Julia

1
BEING WELSH

Flag

My Wales

Male voice Choir

Christmas Carols

I suppose being Welsh means different things to different people, but to me it's a pride thing. My maiden name Leyshon is a very old Welsh name and I know that somehow, I go back a very long way. But most of my direct ancestors came to the valleys when the pits were sunk and so are from Cornwall, Yorkshire, and Gloucestershire. That doesn't make me any less Welsh.

These communities were full of the pride that we today see as "Welsh". I am a Valley girl (my car registration plate says so!) and the valley is part of me.

And to this day when I see my country's flag flying on the T.V. or in a New Zealand garden (which has prompted me on at least one occasion to knock on the door...) I get very patriotic. So, if you are Welsh too, I expect you feel the same.

Wales is known as the land of song. We talk in sing-song voices and our voices go up at the end of a sentence. We all sing the National Anthem till our hearts might burst whenever we get the chance. Tom Jones is ours, as is Catherine Jenkins and Charlotte Church, and let's not forget Shirley whatsername....!

And song is not song without a male voice choir- in my opinion the epitome of Welsh sound. You hear it and your mind is instantly transported back, wherever you are in the world. The sound of miners coming home after a day's slog, the sound of the chapel on Sunday, Christmas Day or a man's funeral as they bring him home... It is the sound of the heavens to me, and as they lower me into the ground it will, God-willing, be the last sound I ever hear.

Flag

Up flies the Dragon

High in the sky

Backed with white and green.

A true sight for the eye,

He is red with claws of death.

He looks toward home.

He faces west

West.to my country, and those I love.

Breathing fire from high above

He strikes fear into the feeble hearts

Of those who would set us far apart.

They don't know the dragon's fearsome breath

Powers our hearts in life, and beyond death

So fly my dragon, spread your wings

And as I watch you...

...my heart sings

My Wales

What do I think of this land, my Wales?

A land of magic and elven tales

Of mystery and dragon breath

Of castles, and battles fought to death

A land of songs sung sweet and loud

A land where poor men stand up proud

A land of coal that men did haul

A land that worships a rugby ball

A land that welcomes and enfolds

Its countrymen, a land that holds

Its people in its coal scarred heart

Whether safe at home or far apart

One day once more I wish to see

The land that made and moulded me

A hiraeth burns far across the world

My land still calls to this proud Welsh girl…

St. David's Day

March one, march all
March into the assembly hall
Little girls decked in welsh hats
Little boys in their flat caps

Leeks and daffodils proudly pinned
As the children gather within
Take a breath to swell the lungs
Ready for hymns to be sung

The choir of a hundred children might
Be likened to that of a dragon in flight
Swirling, beating, it reaches a roar
And always, always, still there is more

Land of my Fathers their battle cry
As the dragon red soars in the sky
Mothers weep at the sound
Of heaven's voice, here on the ground

March one, March all
For St David's Day in the school assembly hall.

Male Voice Choir

I have been a good girl all my life
Tried to show kindness and stood to each test
And Heaven is where I shall go to end my strife
And the Valley is my Heaven- it's where I would rest

No Angels in white gowns to sit on high
With harps and snow-white feathers on their wing
No heavenly voices with exalted sighs
No- I want to hear a male voice choir sing

As I return to earth as we all must
I'll listen to "Mwfanwy" soft and low
The voices of Welsh men, good men I trust
To ease my passing as on my way I go

They'll sing "Land of my Fathers", "Calon Lan"
And raise my soul to Heaven, ever higher
My friend, no angel has, and never can
Sound as heavenly as a Welsh male voice choir

Christmas Carols

In junior school I learned to sing
I learned the hymns so well
And as we sang in assembly
My heart would start to swell

Our teacher, Mr Williams
Always dressed in shirt and tie
Waved his baton towards us
As if reaching for the sky

We sang our little hearts out
We would give it our all
He always got the best of us
With every rise and fall

All November we would practice
Till we sang as one pure voice
Then late in December
Finally, time to rejoice

Into Saron chapel
Trouped every girl, every boy
In the wooden balcony
To sing of Christmas joy

All the Christmas Carols
Would be tackled one by one
Until the very last
Which was by far the most fun

Called the Cowboy Carol
It told of new starts
And when we all sang "Ya Yippee!"
I felt the music swell my heart

The old chapel, in that service
I swear would be raised
As our village congregation
Sang our songs of Christmas praise

Welsh people and Christmas Carols
An old chapel and a night of song
A memory to cherish
My whole life long.

Julia Scanlon

2
RUGBY

Merv the Swerve

Not Getting the 2011 World Cup

Now a big part of valley pride is tied up in rugby. Major surprise, we love it.

I confess I don't know the rules but just cheer anyway-and of course the ref is always rubbish when we "concede" a match (note the phrasing - we NEVER lose).

I remember being on my paper round and asking the score at every house on match days.

When I finally left home, and lived (gulp!) in England, I also remember going to a Bath vs Northampton match in which my crush, Ieuan Evans, was playing for Bath (my long - suffering English husband has always been understanding of my love for Ieuan).

We had one Bath top and one Northampton top between us. I lost the toss and wore the latter. You can probably guess my husband's embarrassment when Ieuan scored a try...

Another favourite, but when I was much younger, was Mervyn Davies. Merv was one heck of a player in the days when it seemed we couldn't lose.

Below is a rhyme I wrote when he passed away in 2012.

Merv the "Swerve"

When I was a girl, when I was small
I was taught that pride came with a rugby ball
Those were the days when our boys had nerve
To win everything. One was Merv the Swerve.

With his white sweatband, and his massive 'tach
He ruled our field - had a bit of panache
To me he **was** rugby. He was all I knew
As I grew up and my patriotism grew.

One day we heard the news, it was bad
He'd collapsed on the field, brain hurt, we were sad
But we knew in the background that our Merv was still there
Shouting for our boys, sending up a prayer.

And this year our Merv, those prayers they worked
Nearly beat the French, though when we didn't, it irked
You saved the best till last, had a word with God up there
If you didn't get your way, eternity He couldn't bear.

He had to act and so this year we won,
but God- why could you not wait
Until Our Merv had seen us win the Slam –
Before you took our lovely No.8.?

Not Getting the 2011 World Cup

Don't worry that the dragon's died.

He merely sleeps.

Gone to his fiery den, his watch still keeps

Over the country, one eye just half-closed.

Ready to wreak his wrath upon our foes.

Four years he will curl his tail beneath his wing.

Waiting, waiting, waiting for us to sing.

Our song of battle will release his ties

And send him soaring o'er enemies skies.

He is merely biding time until the day

Our boys in red can finally get their way.

He can afford to wait a measly four-

But watch him then... and hear his fire roar...

3
MINING

Of course, the Rhondda wouldn't be the Rhondda without its mining history. When the first pit was sunk news travelled fast and a lot of miners and their families arrived to take advantage of ready work. It wasn't pleasant work, but it kept food on the table and a roof over heads.

My grandfather, Glyndwr Llewelyn Leyshon, was a miner and died from lung complications. The family believe it was pneumoconiosis, however this was denied, and they received no compensation (incidentally, pneumoconiosis was the first word I read in the newspaper to my father- I loved words even at five).

On my mother's side my great grandfather William Semmens, was an immigrant from Cornwall, with a long mining history.

My grandfather (Bampi) Morgan Griffiths, escaped that fate- he was encouraged to do something else and was an engineer, working on aircraft at St. Athens air force base and was an artist in his spare time. I am so thankful that my father was also spared pit work.

The valleys are making a comeback since the closure of the pits- I am not there to see it but my friends post pictures and it looks wonderful. One day I will see it again.

Slag heaps were near every village in the Rhondda Valleys, and when I looked up the valley as a child I would see Tylorstown tip in the distance- in my innocence I thought it was a volcano, and it did indeed garner the nickname of "Old Smokey".

It has since been levelled to make it safer, as have most of the slag heaps, following the Aberfan disaster. Much bitterness remains, but that is for debate elsewhere.

The 50th anniversary of the Aberfan disaster was commemorated in 2016. I was tiny when this happened, but we were brought up to never forget it. Although not the Rhondda, it could have so easily been any village nearby, and the tragedy is held in the hearts of us all. In this small village, my entire generation (they would only be a few years older than me) was entirely wiped out. I have included a poem to commemorate the disaster, and hope that lessons were learned so we never have something like this happen again.

To Make Men Rich

A pit was sunk, to mine for coal
To make men rich from hell's black gold.
Their workers came from far, and wide
To crawl down deep, as if to hide.
To chip away at the valley floor
To make men rich, yet more, yet more.

And green began to disappear
As pit by pit, the black grew near.
Smoke blanketed the valley from blue sky
Wherever you looked, a pit was nigh.
Jewelled landscape faded to grey
To make men rich each weary day

Grey houses, perched like dominos
Above the valley floor arose.
Housing that was quick and cheap
Nestled under slurry heap.
Stone hacked out of Nature's hills
To make men rich She endured such ills.

The pits did their job, and did it well
As workers did their stint in hell.
As children died under slag heaps
Because the rich men wanted "cheap".
And so, it went that poor men mined coal
To make men rich - which was their goal.

Those days are gone now, green returns
To the valleys for which my heart burns.
The rivers recovered, the waters clear
The fish came back after many years.
Mother Nature has finally wielded her sword.
To make us rich, green valleys, our reward

Pit

The wheel turns, and we go down
Ever deeper, into the ground.
They got it wrong, in that book of old.
There are no fires burning mister, Hell is cold.

Crammed like sardines inside the cage
There I see young Davey, young, in age.
Sixteen just yesterday was our Dave.
Lord, let not this pit become his early grave.

Reaching the bottom, I adjust my pack
And spilling out like ants, we walk into the black.
Feeling my way, I turn on my lamp
And hope with all my heart, that there is no firedamp.

Chipping away, stones hit my skin.
A blue-black mark, telling where I've been.
Every day my cough gets a bit worse
But I hope it'll be years afore I'm in my hearse.

The foreman calls out to stop to eat-
I pull out my package of bread and meat.
Most days it is merely bread and jam.
Today I am a lucky man.

Back to my toil I go, hacking the seam.
As I pick out the coal, I let myself dream
Of going up to the top again
Where waits my beautiful wife, Gwen.

She is light in my dark, peace to my toil
Calm to my dreams, grass to my soil.
I think of young Dewi, still wrapped in the shawl
And the dinner that's waiting, a nice pot of cawl.

And to go with it, an enormous chunk of bread.
Clean sheets on the line, fresh pillow for my head.
A cup of tea and a Welsh cake
That on the stone today she would bake.

The hooter blows, and we line up for the ride
All anxious to be the first inside.
Rising from the deep quiet, to light and noise
Making plans to sup ale with the boys.

Laughing, joking, relieved once again
We stop being rats in the dark, once more are men.
Thank you God, I'll put a penny on the plate on Sunday
And be back to work another day on Monday

Old Smokey

For years he's sat majestic over the town
Watching ant-like men as he looks down
Black, foreboding, threatening looming high.
Made by Man, he rules the valley's sky

Darkly steaming, volcano-like with his peak.
Strong, unyielding presence, never meek.
When thunder rolls and blackens clouds above
The village wonders if Old Smokey's on the move.

In fear, they look up towards the hills
See his outline swell and fear the ills
That he will wreak upon good men
If such a thing would happen once again

But for now, the skies become clear
And so again, away rushes our fear
And Old Smokey once again will sleep
And over the towns his watch will quietly keep

His summit now removed, his temper calmed
And Man, at long last feels safe from harm
Grassed slopes give peace to us, yet, my friend, yet
When dark clouds come- we still remember Smokey's threat…

The Last Day of School

Mammy do I have to go to school today?
Yes love, you do, it's not too far away.
The walk will do you good and then
When you get there you can play with your friends.

So off I pop down the road to Pantglas
It's cold outside, the sky is looking overcast
The fog has settled over the street
And I look down, it is wet under my little feet.

Never mind I shall soon be in the warm
Sat at my desk I shall come to no harm
I will sit quietly and learn my ABC's
And in just a few hours it's half term- I'll run free.

I reach the school, I'm just in time
For register, it's just on nine.
Miss is now calling our names out.
Why is she suddenly starting to shout?

I hear the noise, as we assemble
And the floor begins to creak and tremble.
Rumbling louder, suddenly- CRACK!
And just like that my world is black.

Oh, Mam, where are you? I can't see!
Can you look, can you please find me?
Oh dear, I think that I am gone
And I have left you all alone...

They buried us upon a hill.
It's peaceful there, quiet, still
Silent, where there should be noise
Of happy girls and scampering boys.

Though 50 years has now gone by
You can still hear those mammies cry.
Each dad was left a broken man
The price of coal was too high, at Aberfan...

Julia Scanlon

4
CHURCH AND CHAPEL

Penuel

Over the wall

Most children in our community went to Sunday school, whether you were Baptist, Church of England or other. I was duly dispatched every Sunday to Penuel. We generally sat in the little back room, and I can remember it being quite small. Only occasionally we were allowed in the chapel itself, and it was quite grand to a small girl. It was quiet and imposing, but beautiful. My neighbour, Hilary got married there in the 1970's, and I was bridesmaid. I remember being so proud of my powder blue dress and white tights that Mam had trouble getting me to get into my pyjamas at the end of the day. Sunday school to me was synonymous with the annual trip to Barry Island. I can remember as a teen when I was trying to find my independence, I abandoned Penuel for a season, preferring to go to another church. The trip for this church coincided with Penuel's, and when I got to the beach at Barry Island I found we were expected to pray on the beach all day. I came back on the Penuel bus with Mam and my brothers! My transgression was never judged and Penuel welcomed me back into the fold…

St Anne's Church was Church of England and I didn't get to go there very often. It was more traditional in its construction, and had larger grounds, not much but the chapels tended to be right on the road- Penuel only had a tiny frontage. I really did dream of marrying "over the wall" but as I moved to England and married a Catholic it wasn't to be- although I did have a nice church wedding.

Penuel

Every Sunday morning was when I would go to chapel
With my penny for collection and a bright and shiny apple
We'd sit down in the vestry and we'd learn about our Lord
(In truth, because I was so young, I often would be bored)

The wooden pews were polished, and they'd always smell of wax
And so straight they'd make us wriggle, not comfy for our backs
We'd learn "The Good Samaritan" and Daniel in the Den
Delilah and her Samson with the strength of many men

My favourite time was Christmas and the Nativity
I wanted to be Mary- but Miss never would pick me
It was held in the main chapel with its balcony all around
And when we sang our carols You'd appreciate the sound

The organist would strike a note and get us into tune
And I would sing my heart out in this old oak cladded room.
Harvest time we'd bring along a little food donation
And at the altar there would be a beautiful creation…

Made of bread with golden crust and shaped like ears of wheat
Just tempting little six- year olds to break a piece to eat!
But we all knew that loaf of bread that graced the Holy stage
Was not for little girls or boys, it was for the old aged

Anniversary came around and with it- recitation!

Memorising bible verse Caused angst and great frustration

And when the day arrived, and we were put up to the test

Our mothers would escort us each dressed up in Sunday best

With hair in bows, faces scrubbed, new white socks and sandals

We'd puff our chests to kid ourselves we're big enough to handle

The important job of saying the poem, song or verse

That every child had taken several weeks to rehearse

Our trip to Barry Island Was the payment for our pain

On big red buses, we would climb to see the sea again

We'd sing some songs and eat our sweets till "Drive" would shout

That they had spied the ocean then the kids would all peer out

We'd park up near the station and we'd head off to the prom

Making note of the number of the bus that we'd come from

Mam would set a deckchair or a towel on the sand

I'd pop up to the toilet, that in Barry was very grand!

I'd spend my penny then I'd read the older kids' graffiti

It really wasn't nice but at my age I found it witty!

Then back down to the beach to slather Nivea on my skin

And wash it off straight after, with a salty sandy swim

Later to the fairground on the ghost train and Helter- Skelter

While Mam went in to Bingo, claiming that she was seeking shelter

Candy floss and cockles, Doughnuts rock and ice cream

Rendered us, if not sick, then at least bursting at the seam

At last we'd head off to the bus with our mam and dad

Claiming that this years' trip was "the best we've ever had"

Belting out in unison that we'd never want to roam

As we sang our home time favourite song…

"Show me the way to go home"

These are just some memories of my childhood, sweet and free

They may be rose-tinted, but they are what made me, *me*

I am all grown now but those young years, they served me well

I believe I'm blessed to have a place like Penuel

Over the Wall

Though I was "Welsh Chapel"
It always seemed to me
That when I was to marry
St Anne's it was to be.

Every Saturday morning
Especially summertime
We would race on over
At the first bell's chime.

Mothers in their curlers
All would happily amble
Kids would tag along too
Hoping for a "scramble".

We'd climb upon the wall
To get a better view
And at the bride's arrival
We all would "Ah!" and "Ooh!".

She'd pause a little moment
Amid baby's breath and rose
And then the organ sounded
And they'd open the big doors.

A little shake of nervousness
A beautiful bright smile
She'd hold on to her Daddy
As he walked her down the aisle.

Although outside 'twas sunny
In church it would be cool
And the sunlight played on the window
Throwing colours around like jewels

Hymns were sung and readings
Would be made by folks and friends
Vows made to each other
That their love would never end

Then out into the sunshine
The couple would emerge
Confetti thrown, abundant
Glistening on the verge

Many happy memories
Were made in old St Anne's
Many marriages started
Between a woman and a man..

Me? I married elsewhere

But I always will recall

The days I'd dream of being

A St. Anne's bride...." over the wall"

5
FOOD

Faggots n Peas

Welsh Cakes

Cawl

Welsh people love their food and Rhondda people are no different. For me, certain foods bring back memories of times past. For example, an early memory is of staying with my grandmother (Mams Leyshon) on a Sunday, and for Sunday tea would be tinned peaches and bread and butter- which she would duly dunk in the juice. Sounds horrendous but it was delicious, Similarly, my Nanna Griffiths would tell us to save the doughboy from the *cawl*- then dollop jam on for pudding. I suppose it was a way of saving money. Cream puffs remind me of my "Aunty" Margaret (my next- door neighbour- to a child all adults are Aunty or Uncle in Welsh culture) as she always took me to Ponty market just before Christmas to buy presents for the family and would take me to Prince's Café. My family always got nicer presents than I could really afford- I think Margaret would sort of "add" to my savings somewhat! She would also buy me the "Diana" annual for Christmas every year. 1977 was the year she died - I received my annual duly on Christmas Day-she had purchased it months before. I will never forget her.

But I digress- I was trying to lead you to Ponty Market, and the faggots and peas…

Faggots and peas were a big part of growing up although I never remember them as part of Mam's repertoire. They were a pure indulgence on a visit to Ponty Market. Anyone from the Rhondda reading this will be probably familiar with the market.

Stalls selling towels, fabric, hardware and food, arranged through a cobbled street with an indoor part where you'd find butchers, florists etc. And it was in this indoor bit that they sold the faggots and peas.

Cheap and filling, they were very popular, especially on a chilly day, and usually followed with cake and custard. I love faggots and peas but living away from home it is impossible to get them, although I have had a try at making some with a passable result.

Faggots and Peas

I sit in my house, and I see the rain
And my mind begins to drift again
To rainy days in Pontypridd,
The market, and the faggots and peas.

As soon as the rain would fall to the ground,
We'd head to the indoor café to sit down
Raincoats steaming, dripping wet
Looking forward to what we'd get.

Formica tables and plastic chairs
Lined in a row, waiting there
While Mam ordered I'd find a seat
And wait impatiently for my treat.

First the triangles of white bread
On little plates to us would head
And then the small white Pyrex dishes
Filled with the thing to fulfil our wishes.

Savoury, meaty, a hint of spice
Covered in gravy, oh, so nice
Fat soft peas, of vivid green
Waiting for us to wipe bowls clean.

Vinegar to sprinkle in

A pauper's dish fit for any king

Accompanied with hot, strong tea

To warm us through, my Mam and me.

I'd dip my bread in, slow at first

But waiting made me fit to burst

Soon eating as if 'twere my last meal

So good did that little dish make me feel.

And soon the bowl again was white

As I cleaned it with the bread, took my last bite

Hoping Mam would think I deserved

To get a little second serve.

And finally, we'd finish up.

Our tea we'd drink in a last big sup

And head on out the frosted glass door

To brave the rain a little more.

My memories are now a distant haze

But I often think about market days

That love and nurturing from my mother

Took the form of faggots- with gravy over....

Welsh cakes

Heaven is a Welsh Cake, warm from the griddle
Golden on the outside, fluffy in the middle
Speckled with some currants, a little mixed spice
On any day of the week, nothing is as nice

Every Saturday afternoon, out would come the flour
And I would watch Mam happily, for about an hour
Into the bowl would go the flour, eggs, sugar fat and milk
And then she'd mix and knead until the dough resembled silk

Dough would be on everything, even her nose and hair
But we were getting Welsh Cakes, who on earth would care?
Out would come the pop bottle, with icy water in
To get the pastry thin enough (she had no rolling pin).

Cutting with a teacup, making little rounds
Dropping on the pan, they would make a sizzle sound.
Then she'd flip them over to cook the other side
Finally, ready, and onto a plate they'd slide

Poetry From the Coal

Dusted with some sugar, to make them extra sweet

And then came silence as we all would begin to eat

To make a ton of Welsh Cakes would take Mam so long

And within twenty minutes the entire lot was gone

Never would Mam's Welsh Cakes last for more than a day

And as she reached for the crumbs she'd sigh as she'd hear us say

"With a hot cup of tea to wash it down the hatch

Mam, Heaven is a Welsh Cake- *so come on, cook another batch!*"

Cawl

Come inside my child
For winter's very cold
Warm your hands at the fire
I will get you a bowl

Sit at the table my child
Your tummy must be empty
But Nanna has made *Cawl*
And in the pot, there's plenty

Lift your spoon my child
And take a bite or two
I've added lots of veg
And a chunk of lamb for you

Break your bread my child
Let nothing go to waste
Dip it in the broth
Revel in the taste

Eat your fill my child
Till you can hardly move
For a bowl of Welsh *Cawl*
Is full, with Nanna's love

Julia Scanlon

6
FAMILY

A Day out with my Dwd

The Day "Mams" became a Criminal

Nanna and Bampi's Infamous Picnic

They say it takes a village to raise a child. This is true of the valleys of my childhood. All children were able to play and grow, knowing that they were relatively safe (at least from people, maybe not railways!) with prying eyes of the neighbours ever near, to watch out for and sometimes scold them. I had many family members scattered about, aunties and uncles, older cousins too.

But the people who were most important to me after my Mam, Dad and brothers were my grandparents. "Mams" and "Dwd" (Gwenllyn and Glyndwr Leyshon) lived in *Trebanog*, at the top of the mountain. Dwd died when I was little, but I still remember his face, and his kindness and love. Mam told me he would walk every Saturday down to *Ynyshir* and back just to see his grandchildren. Such was his love. I remember the incident with the "gows" although I was little at the time. It is my lasting treasure.

And my Mams! Now there was a pillar of the community. I remember her teaching me to crochet and staying with her through the summer. My cousin Alyson who lived next door to her would sit with me out back on an old car seat that was propped against the back wall and we would make Sindy clothes.

We would have meals at her kitchen table which was covered in sticky-backed plastic with pictures of fruit on it, and on Sundays our tea would be tinned peaches and bread and butter. Mams was as skinny as a rake, and always wore a mustard coloured, flowery button through housecoat. She would let us watch her black and white TV while eating the peaches. Her chairs and settee filled the tiny room. She lived a very lonely life when Dwd was gone, a very quiet one.

A law-abiding lady. Or was she ?...

A Day Out with my Dwd

Many years ago. you passed
And my memory is fading fast
But the day you took me over to "Ton"
My Dwd, that memory lingers on

I was all of six, if even that
When you donned your faithful old Dai cap
Swung me on your shoulders so high
Till I almost felt I touched the sky

A pack of sandwiches we sealed
In brown paper before we crossed the field
It was sunny as we left *Henllys*
And headed over past the trees

Across a stile and into battle!
(For I was so afraid of cattle)
"Oh Dwd! There's GOWS!" I cried in fear
"Don't worry child, for I am here"

You answered. "Just hold your head high
And they'll just let you walk on by".
Doing as my grandad told
Made it alright, it made me bold

And through I walked, a brave girl now

Over that field, past every "gow"

And on to *Tonyrefail* town

Where we found a place, and sat ourselves down

Ate our packed lunch without a care

It was better than any fancy fare

Nothing can ever taste so good

As a sandwich shared with the world's best Dwd

Not too long after, when I was seven

Your presence was required in Heaven

I have had to grow up all these years

Learning, without you, to face my fears

But I still do as I am told

That little child, though not very bold

I hold my head and my "gows" disappear

As if they know that you're still near

And though the years go by I won't let go

Of my lovely Grandad, I loved so

With your love around me I'll get by

I'll even learn to touch the sky.

The Day "Mams" Became a Criminal

My Mams taught me right from wrong
That good girls go to Heaven
But Mams had a very dark secret
That I found out when I was seven

You see Mams was a criminal
Had fallen foul of the law
The black sheep of the family
Like no one ever before

What was the crime committed?
Did she poison, maim or stab?
Did she break into some houses?
Did she perform a "smash and grab"?

Was she a lady Godfather?
With a cut off horse's head?
Did she hold someone to ransom?
Or shoot somebody dead?

Well, it all began one Sunday
On the worksite up the road
All the men around were stealing
Building supplies by the carload

Gravel, concrete, bricks and plaster
All considered to be fair game
Yes, the building site was the crime scene
Where she'd hang her head in shame

For Mams' pot plant was waterlogged…
And needed a little sand
So off she went up the road
Children's bucket, and spade in hand

But Mams was unaware that day
That the police were on the prowl
And as she dug a spade-full
Blue lights flashed, the siren howled

The game was up, the thief was caught
Red-handed (if a little sandy)
The wails of our poor Mams
Were heard from here to *Tonypandy*

Dad was at the gate as Mams
Was frog-marched to the door
Trembling like a leaf and head
Cast down towards the floor

The policeman tried to hide his smile
As Mams was ushered in
And made to tell the sorry tale
And confess to the sin

Let off with a caution
She bid the policeman farewell
And off he went to the station
His gleeful tale to tell

Of the Godmother of *Trebanog*
The scariest criminal of all
The lady with the plastic spade-
And kids bucket from Porthcawl….

Of course, I had two sets of grandparents, and I also spent a lot of time with my Mam's parents, Morgan and Doris Griffiths (Mog and Dolly). Mog, or Bampi to me, was very creative, and spent many a happy hour painting landscapes in the bedroom of their tiny two up two down home in Mary Street, Porth.

Bampi had a facial palsy from an early age and one side of his face drooped a little, but he never let it get him down. He had the most infectious laugh that was a little like how you'd imagine Santa to laugh. Nanna was extremely strait laced and Bampi would tease her mercilessly.

They met as he was walking by one day, and he gave her a rose and asked to court her, which was very romantic. They loved each other deeply. Although we did all wonder if they would make it to their Golden wedding anniversary as they were threatening to divorce each other two weeks before. But celebrate they did, and their Diamond, before cancer took him just before my son's first birthday.

They led a simple but happy and fun life, and in the early days had a motorbike and sidecar, and Bampi would take Nanna to the countryside to go on romantic walks…

Nanna and Bampi's Infamous Picnic

Nanna got left some money
Nearly fifty pounds
And bought a motorbike and sidecar
So her and Bamp could get around

She always told us later
It was the best money she spent
As every weekend in summer
To the country they went

Nan always wore trousers
Whether the sky was grey or blue
And for this there was a good reason
Which I now can relate to you

Nanna was a smart lady
And liked to make herself nice
Because she loved our Bampi
And that loving look in his eyes

So in the early days of courtship
A hundred strokes she would give her tresses
Put her best lipstick on
And always wear beautiful dresses

On this particular occasion

The morning came, sunny and bright

So Nanna made a decision

She had to look just right

A summer dress came out of the wardrobe

Silk stockings, soft and new

All set to make an impression

On Bampi, her forever beau

Tootling off to the country

With a picnic and a flask of tea

Oh what a lovely adventure

This was about to be!

They parked at a field near *Llantwit*

And set to walk down the track

If Nanna had known what would happen

She would've turned and walked back

Now Bamp was a bit of a prankster

And had walked to the spot before

He started to hang back a little

Chuckling at what was in store

"Come on Doll, I'll help you get over"
He turned to Nan with a smile
And with the cunning of a croc in the water
He helped her over the stile

A few minutes later she was screeching
Baying for Bampi's blood
For Nan and her expensive silk stockings
Were up to her knickers in mud

The sandwiches went for a burden
The flask of tea went quite cold
Nanna went for him with the basket
And with a dragons tongue she did scold

They went back to the valley in silence
And didn't hold hands for a while
But soon Nanna saw the funny side
And in time she was able to smile

They spent sixty years as a couple
Lived, loved, laughed and danced
But we'll always remember the date
That showed just who wore the pants!

Julia Scanlon

7
PLACES

Up the hill to *Llanwonno*

Porth baths

Dan Dicks Quarry

Most of my childhood was spent at the park or up the mountains. Living in the foothills of the mountains gave us plenty of space to run around. We didn't usually walk all the way to the top but stayed close to home.

There were cob nut trees to raid, streams to float sticks on, tadpoles to see, and freedom to try it all out. My Mam said she did more trekking up the hills than we ever did but I think we did alright really! When we weren't running amok on the side of a hill we could spent summer at the baths in Porth. The poem about the pool is based on a true event, and I thank the lad that pushed me for my love of swimming today. I am not one of life's exercise fiends, but I do love a swim.

These days the pools are mainly indoors, and I give thanks that we can now swim all year round, but a part of me hankers to those long summer days splashing around, diving and bombing, and crisps and sandwiches with pop to wash down.

Talking of hot, summer days, a good part would be spent the other side of the valley, trekking up with friends to Dan Dick's Quarry. I never found out why it was called that, but it was an eerie place, just right for your imagination to run wild...

Up the hill to *Llanwonno*

I remember walks with Mam
Oh, so very long ago
Heading up the mountain
Towards *Llanwonno*

The road was straight and narrow
Till the old farm ruin was found
Then became more winding
With gravel on the ground

We'd stop and look behind us
See the village far beneath
And sit upon a rock
To rest and take a breath

Mam would bring a sandwich
To eat as we took a break
And if she had been baking
Maybe a Welsh cake

And then onwards and upwards
As if towards the sky
All the while Mam pointed
To the nature we passed by

Perhaps a clump of frog spawn

In a little mountain pond

Or maybe a rabbit hole,

Or winberries, on the ground

We'd clamber on the stile

Go along a tree-lined path

And not too much further

Was St..Gwynno's church at last

Mam would show us the church

And the grave of *Guto Nythbran*

The man who beat the kettle

The most famous running man

And by this time, we'd be shattered

And our legs were almost bandy

So, to the pub over the road we'd saunter

For crisps and a shandy

All fed, watered and rested

We began the journey back

Singing about "wandering

About the mountain track"

Now I'm older and wiser
And arthritis claimed my knees
I look back with so much fondness
On summer days such as these

So, my friend while you are young
If there is somewhere you want to go
Ditch the car- take the high road
I promise you'll love *Llanwonno*

Porth Baths

Summer started early
In the valleys of my youth
Of course, I'm being sarcastic
It was bloody cold, in truth

But never mind the drizzle
Or the wind, or the driving hail
June was "swimming lessons"
Never mind how much we'd wail

Up to Porth baths we'd venture
With our bathers in a towel
Into the freezing change-room
So cold that we would howl

Arms across our chests
To keep the cold from getting through
Nothing worked and so
Our fingers and toes would be quite blue

Lined up in a row
We would swim towards the bar
Two strokes and a bubble
Three feet is so bloody far!

Then you'd take a breath
Just as you shouldn't flippin' oughter
And take a fly-filled mouthful
Of "pure" chlorinated water

With so many children
The worry wasn't that we'd drown
We'd be more concerned
About code yellow-or worse, brown!

I was a hopeless case and so
Failed at every session
But then when I was twelve I got
A real-life swimming lesson.

The first day of the holidays
I got pushed in the deep end
Saw my short life in front of me
I could swear I got the bends.

Once comforted at home
By Mam, who once swam for her school
My real lesson began with her
At that same bloody pool

Till finally six weeks later

From the top board I could dive

I was a fully-fledged swimmer

The best swimmer alive!

And all those years since then

I've found my love for swimming grew

All for getting pushed

Into Porth pool- cold, fly-filled and blue…

Dan Dicks Quarry

With a packet of crisps and fizzy pop
We'd set off in a crowd
Just kids having a good time
Maybe a little wild and loud

Beating our way through the bracken
Trying to watch for grass snakes
We'd be more likely to scare them skinless
With the noise us kids would make

Flies and bees buzzing around us
In the summer heat
As we slowly climbed the mountain
The fresh air would smell warm and sweet

And at last we'd reach our quarry
The destination, our goal
Where even in mid - summer
It would feel so very cold

Where every little whisper
Sounded like a shout
And after every footstep
An echo sounded out

Listen! There's a noise!

It could just be the breaking of sticks

But let's not wait-get out of here

Let's find somewhere else for a picnic

They say the place was haunted

Who am I to say they're wrong

We never found out the truth

Because we never stayed too long...

Julia Scanlon

8
THINGS

Often, it's the possessions we have that bring back the memories. Like your new-born baby's first outfit, or the hand- made ornament they brought you to put on the Christmas tree. They are often not perfect, but they hold so much love and memory in them you just can't get rid of them. In this throw away age I wonder what we will do to jog our memories.

In the Rhondda, we have many "things" that are traditional, such as the Welsh Love Spoon and the Welsh Shawl.

Both to me symbolize love, in all its forms. I must be honest here and say that I don't own a shawl, but I do remember Mam nursing my brothers in a green and white check blanket in the Welsh fashion, and Nanna appears in a picture with me as a baby in a shawl.

Later as I grew I remember Mam in the street cuddling the neighbours' babies in a flannelette sheet- anything would do, it was the comfort that mattered…

My Dad has always been someone that liked to make things. Although he found it difficult to find regular work, and later became ill with depression, he has always had a shed, lathe etc., and put in his own kitchen when I was younger.

I vaguely remember holding a bit of wood for him to saw from time to time. He went to various occupational therapy sessions because of his health issues, and carved me my Love Spoon at one of those sessions.

He still has his shed, and although we try to discourage him at 73 from working there (on the grounds of Health and Safety!) he still potters.

He currently has an extensive model train collection and has lately decided to start on model boats. My long-suffering mother just rolls her eyes…

The Welsh Shawl

Today I cleaned my closet, of all that was within
Most of it was rubbish, fit only for the bin
I pulled out pillowcases that didn't have a pair
Old sheets and duvet covers -threw them out without a care

And as I continued my cleaning, my hands began to tug
On a piece of woollen fabric- maybe an old rug?
It was right at the back of the cupboard, jammed in very tight
So I gathered all my strength and pulled with all my might

And out of the closet it tumbled.
A blanket, checked in white and green
Stained with age, and threadbare. The sorriest sight I've ever seen.
The bin bag was duly opened and in it was made to drop
When amidst all my efforts something made me stop

And I sat down exhausted at that cupboard in my hall
And thought about that fabric- my old Welsh nursing shawl
That once belonged to Nanna when it was new and fine
Washed fresh every Monday and hung out on the line

Handed down to Mammy, who walked me up the street

Tucked up nice and cosy. from my head to my feet.

She nursed us through the measles, teething, fevers, and all

With a mother's never - ending love and that old Welsh shawl

We took it up the mountain on picnics in the hills

That stain in the right-hand corner is from blackcurrant,

that we spilled.

To Barry Island that old shawl accompanied us each year

And suffered from the sand, and Dad's occasional bottled beer.

With time and use it faded, with each child a new hole darned

We didn't have much money, so Mam used the cheapest yarn

With each trip we lost some fringing, or a little bit got torn

But each Monday still it got washed, ready for the next new-born

I visited Mam with my babies, and right from the very first

They were paraded up the street, in that shawl they too were nursed

The pride on Mammy's face, she would have such a ball

Swaying from side to side with her grand-kid in that shawl.

It was only a scrap of fabric, barely six feet square

But the memories of generations were woven right in there

With faded green wool, and its patches- and that damned

blackcurrant stain

How could I get rid of it so easily? No, it must remain

So, I reached inside the bin bag and again began to pull
Feeling the warmth and comfort of a lifetime wrapped in wool.
I got the tub all ready, it was Monday, the day was fine
And that bloody shawl got washed…

… and hung up proudly on my line.

Love Spoon

On the wall in my lounge is an old wooden spoon
It's been years since 'twas carved, many a moon
Barely twelve inches, not worth much in gold
But its riches are many, for the love that it holds

It's a light- coloured wood and is simple in looks
Not intricate like the ones you see in books
Just two small hearts, no inscription you'll find
But it's very special, for it is all mine

It didn't take long for it to be made
I don't know if he even needed a lathe
There are marks where the chisel slipped out of his hand
And scarred the soft wood, like a pit scars the land

The hearts are lopsided and not even- sized
But they are just perfect, seen through my eyes
For the hearts are as big as the ocean to me
I care not a jot for what others see

It wouldn't stir *Cawl,* to make a good dinner
In a spoon competition, it would never be winner
But that tiny wee spoon, hewn out of pine
Was made by the one man that's always been mine

Most spoons are made by a boy for his sweet

To impress her and show that her needs he can meet

But my spoon was made by the very best carver

A girl could have – and that was my father

He wasn't young when he took to his shed

His hands slightly shaky, would slip, and they bled

To carve those wee hearts for his only girl

So that spoon to me is the whole wide world

It's only some wood – a bit wonky in parts

A bowl, a stem, and two lopsided hearts.

But when my Dad gave me that chisel-scarred spoon

He gave me his heart- it's worth more than the moon.

9
LIVING DAY TO DAY

Ty Bach

Bath time

A Miner's Wife

The Coal Train

The Sioni Wynwyns Man

Ablutions and other things...

I barely remember it, but I must have had an outside toilet for a good portion of my childhood.

My parents, as did many families living in the terraced houses that were home to Valley people, received a grant in the early to mid-seventies, to make their house more habitable.

A new bathroom and kitchen was added, and we had central heating for the first time. The front room and "living room" were knocked through.

I remember the day Elvis died, hearing the news on the radio, and I remember that day we still had two different carpets front and back, with a strip of concrete in between where the wall was.

Don't ask me why I remember it, but it places the work firmly in 1977, so I was 12 when I had an inside bathroom!

My bathroom was a delightful shade of warm beige called "Sun King" and my Dad (in his infinite wisdom) decided to tile the walls black.

Add a shower curtain in sky blue and you have the stuff of dreams!

To add insult to injury, the plans were incorrect, and the drainage was in before anyone realised.

Thus, we were to have one of the biggest bathrooms in the street- and the smallest kitchen...

I still remember the backyard toilet, or *Ty Bach* (little house) as it is affectionately known.

Ty Bach

Off down the back to Ty Bach in the night
Holding my head high, trying not to show my fright
I'm crossing my poor legs and trying to smile
It can't be twenty paces, yet it feels like a mile

Pulling up the latch, peering inside
Trying to think of places where a spider might hide
I've got a little torch-it shows right where he lays
Duw, I hope I'm fast before I become his next prey

Sitting down on the seat, nearly screeching in pain
Winter's very cold, the seat's frozen once again
My nighty's very thin and made of cheap cotton
No protection for a partly frozen bottom

Thank goodness! No mishaps, I'm very soon done
We're out of toilet paper so it's strips of "The Sun"
Dad came down earlier so it's lucky for me
I got a decent read tonight, he's taken page three

Pulling things together I pull the chain to flush
Feeling reassured I exit in a rush
Nighty tucked into my nicks, done in such a hurry
But that's not the problem, that tickle makes me worry…

Julia Scanlon

Running up the backyard, on my little feet

I look down with my torch- and my nightmare's complete

As I see Mr Spider has made an attack

Two legs went to Ty Bach, ten legs came back….

Bath time

On the back of the house was my old tin bath
Suspended on a rusty nail
Brought in once a week in front of the hearth
Filled to the brim with a pail

Dad would go first then down the rank
That was the way
By the time Mam got in, the water stank
And was cold, greasy and grey

The soap was the cheap stuff, and used as shampoo
It stung our little eyes
Complaining was useless, there was nothing we could do
A fresh bucket would drown out our cries

A scrubbing brush sorted the dirt from our backs
Elbows and grubby knees
We'd wriggle and squirm to avoid the attack
Mammy was deaf to our pleas

And then came the nit-comb to add to our pain
For Mam feared the Nit Nurse
Woe betide if the critters were found in your mane
She would holler and curse

The clippers would follow-Dad would be called
We'd be wrapped tight in a towel
Within a few seconds we'd be horridly bald
As we'd scream, rant and howl

At last, pink from scrubbing, our dignity gone
With not a hair on our head
Nighties and pyjamas were finally put on
And it was up the stairs to bed

The tin bath was emptied and hung on its nail
Ready for next weekend
When the stove was fired up for a hot water pail
And the process begun once again

In seventy- seven our house was modernised
A boiler placed behind the hearth
As hot water on tap poured in front of our eyes
We got rid of that old tin bath

But sometimes when soaking in the tub alone
My eyes mist over and gleam
For I'd swap any amount of sweet smelling foam
To be young, bald, scrubbed pink and clean

A Miner's Wife

Watch her as she works
This miner's wife so proud
Amid all the dirt
Her paving white as a shroud

Watch her as she scrubs
Her little bit 'o' path
Try to step with dirty feet
Watch a dragon's wrath

Watch her red raw hands
From the boiling suds
Back and fore she toils
Removing dust and mud

Watch her as she bends
Down on hands and knees
Strong carbolic soap
Watch her cough and wheeze

Watch her cigarette
In the corner of her lip
Watch her as she tries
Hard not to let it slip

Watch her dowdy clothes
A dirt stained overall
Buttoned to the neck
Darned, and a size too small

Watch this miner's wife
Scrub the pavement down
Until it almost seems
Lower than the ground

Watch this woman well
For she is Welsh. She is pride.
Watch her and love her
For she is what we all are - inside

The Coal Train

Every hour, on the hour
See it trundle past
Count the cars all joined as one
From the first, to the last

Linked by metal, it would grate
As a creaky arthritic joint
Bumping, jolting, painfully
Over the railway points

Up the valley lighter
For it had no load
Down the valley heavy
Filled to brim with black gold

Kids would play round and about
On the smooth track line
Always on the look out
To get out of the way in time

Knowing that it couldn't stop
Living life in fear
Of that dreadful hooting
That signalled it was near

Worried you would trip
And fall to certain death
Kids would cross to the park
Holding their breath

With sighs of relief
As they watch the passing train
Smiles and laughter and fun and games
Till the clock strikes the hour again…

The Sioni Winwns Man

From Brittany he came each year
Face crinkled from the sun
A smile as wide as the channel
The Sioni Winwwns man

As summer came he would appear
With shirt striped white and blue
With a cigarette in his curling lips
He would cycle through

"Will you buy my onions?
Zey are juicy, fat and round"
He would ask each woman nicely
As he rode around the town

So many onions loaded
Upon a bike so small
Hanging from the handlebars
His neck, arms and all

The wives would gather round him
And pay their dues to buy
The best French pink onions
For their cawl, or for a nice pie

At last, his wares offloaded

He would tip his blue beret

Saddle up and pedal

Along his merry way

As summer turned to autumn

Leaves turn to gold and brown

The man with the smile of summer

Returned to his home town

But through the French midwinter

Sowed seeds, and so again began

The yearly "life - cycle"

Of the Sioni Winwwns man

Julia Scanlon

10
SHOPPING

Val and Glan

The Sweetshop

The Butchers

The Bracchi

Fish and chips

Growing up in Ynyshir, I had an array of shops to choose from. Mam would do her shopping locally and daily. From the Top Shop at one end to Val's paper shop at the other, there was a little selection which catered for most needs.

Obviously as a child, my preferences were for the sweetshop. It was called GayShaun's, which was a joining together of the names of the owner's children.

I had a paper round at Val's and they were the kindest people you could know. I spent several years with them, finally becoming a collector, going around getting the weekly payment for the papers. I loved it, but as I also loved chatting to the old people on my way, a Friday evening job became a Friday evening and all day on Saturday. Val was very patient…

Val and Glan

People shape your life in many ways and means
This was just the case from childhood, and through my teens
A couple who helped shape me, and gave me a start
When they gave me my paper round, they took me to their hearts

Proud as punch I'd be, to walk round the back
To reach the wooden bench and to pick up my sack
A little joke from Glan and from Val a wee smile
Wary looks from the dogs, Karl and Helga, all the while

Whatever the weather, warmer or colder
Every day except Sunday that sack was on my shoulder
Off would I saunter, my feet to the ground
Up the road hastily to start my first round

Each newspaper folded carefully into three
Never double the papers, always folded separately
Numbered on the corners with correct destination
This was how I delivered the news of the nation

Then back to the shop to report that I'm done
And a cup of hot cocoa and a biscuit or bun
It was but a simple job, but to a child it still gave
A chance to work hard, a chance to save

Val and Glan taught me the values of an honest day's work

To be willing to try, and never to shirk

They showed me a job where you worked as a team

And after all, isn't that everyone's working dream?

The Sweetshop

Come take a journey back to the old sweet shop
You'll see sights to make your eyes pop
Press your nose to the glass and marvel at jars
Of sweets and gobstoppers and boxes of choc bars

Fireworks and sparklers at Guy Fawkes are displayed
Amid Toffee Apples and dabs wrapped in cellophane, home-
made.
At Christmas when nights draw in early and cold
The fairy lights sparkle on Milk Tray and All Gold

Open the door to the tinkle of bells
Breathe in through your nose and what do you smell?
Aniseed and pear drops, with just a wee hint
Of toffee bonbons, maybe peppermint

From the floor to the ceiling, bottles are stacked
And into the corners crisp boxes are packed
Prawn cocktail and Wotsits and Monster Munch
Fresh and tasty and ready to crunch

Out from the back room comes old Mr. Clements
"Please for a quarter of sherbet lemons
To take home for Dad, Mam would like a Twix,
And for me sir, a ten- penny pick and mix?"

The bags soon filled and bulging inside
Twirled shut by the shopkeeper with ease but with pride
Excitement builds as you exit the place
And head back home at an alarming pace

To find a quiet spot to devote some time
To slurping and chewing your sweeties so sublime
They are all very good and are nearly gone
But the best of course is the very last one!

The old shop was just a window in a two up two down
But it was full of wonder, the talk of the town
For any child with a few pennies to spend
The pull of a sweetshop will never end

The Butcher's Shop

On Saturdays Mam would drag me out for the weekly shop
To the chemist and the green-grocers we'd make a little stop
Fill Mam's bag with goodies and maybe a little treat
But the last stop was the butchers to buy our weekly meat

First, we'd check the window for the offers shown that day
And I'd wonder at the faggots and the pork chops on display
Tucked into a cushion shape were strings of tasty bangers
And usually a lamb leg or a hock strung on a hanger

Stepping in the sawdust made soft landing for our feet
And mingled with the smell of herbs and fresh and tasty meat
The wall tiles were of black and white with animals here and there
And there was a butcher's block where the meat was prepared

Peeping over the counter to get a better look
At the pork and beef carcasses hung on butcher's hooks
It was then I'd see him, smiling, with his apron white and blue
And a snowy trilby on his head- Our friendly butcher Hugh

Mam chooses beef for dinner and to make a cawl, some lamb
But for Saturday tea its salad, so she asks him for some ham
The fresh meat wrapped in paper and put to one side
Out comes the ham hock, With orange breadcrumbs on all sides

He fixes it in place and sets the slicer gauge to thin
Starts it with a flourish, and begins to move it in
Back and forth he toils as he moves the pink meat about
And mesmerised, I watch as the salty slices fall out

A little ham falls, And Hugh puts it to the side
"Want a bit?" "Yes please!" I say and my mouth I open wide
He pops the little bit of ham All juicy, soft and pink
Into my mouth and I chew happily, as he gives a little wink

Mam packs her bag and pays the bill and takes me by the hand
And out we go happily, me still chewing my bit 'o' ham
Mam full of plans for eking out the meagre amount of meat
But with a happy daughter enjoying a little treat

The butchers' shops have now all gone. The supermarkets came.
Their businesses gone under-we all must share the blame
No more ham hocks and sawdust, now our meat is sold on trays
One day, maybe we'll realise- and return to those days

Those days of sausage strings and cured, orange crumbed ham
That filled the belly of many a child, Dad and suffering Mam
Oh, if only we could go back Then maybe time we'd stop
If only we had known the importance of the butcher's shop....

The Bracchi

Step inside the Bracchi Shop
With its red leather seats and Formica table top
Stay awhile- the menu's ample
Plenty of good food to sample

Coffee drips from copper pot
Rich aroma hits the spot
Pungent, strong, yet smooth as brown silk
Ready for the hot-steamed milk

Listen to the pressured steam
Froth the milk to look like cream
Thick and silky, with bubbles on top
Only found in a Bracchi shop

If you're hungry don't be shy
Order a hot steaming pie
Thick gravy poured above
Tasty, meaty, made with love

In summer you could have cream cake
With strawberry or chocolate milkshake
Knickerbocker glory or banana split
Whatever your eyes and tummy saw fit

Or just vanilla ice in a round metal bowl
With raspberry sauce could soothe your soul
A wafer and some nuts on top
All found in the Bracchi shop

No fancy restaurant can compare
To the good honest Italian fare
So, come inside, stay awhile
The Bracchi shop will make you smile

Fish and chips

My memory is taking me on a nostalgic trip
All the way back to Bino's for fish and chips
In my old tired head, I am going back in time
And now all of a sudden, I'm standing in line

Queueing up beside the range, feeling the heat
Looking at the menu board, deciding what to eat
A little board with holes in, half its letters missing
All the while I'm standing I can hear the batter hissing

Fish is turned out on the range, crispy, golden brown
Smacking my lips, mouth waters, the line is going down
Wandering past the pies, sausages and chicken wings
I've made up my mind what to have, today rissole is the king

Fluffy corned beef hash, shaped into balls
Rolled in fresh breadcrumbs, the best bit of all
Placed gently in the fat, in a basket made of wire
Hot steamy delicious, straight out of the fryer

The rissole is ready and with a scoop of golden chips
Served on plate made of newspaper strips
Vinegar from a wooden box with a drippy tap
Was used to fill the bottles, and then on chips it would be slapped

A little salt to season, oh, well really, quite a lot
Hands holding soggy paper, off I would trot
But just as I would begin to walk away
Bino'd give a great big smile and loudly say

"Do you wanta some scrumps? They're a-fresha from-a da pan"
The temptation of crispy bits too much to stand
Eagerly I hand him back my little parcel of chips
And onto the top, a mass of pure gold he slips

Crunchy hot crispiness spills onto the top
And my mouth suddenly waters, it just will not stop
For scrumps and salt and vinegar are food for gods on high
And as close to heaven as food gets for a child such as I

Now I'm getting older and my joints bear the pain
And I try to eat salads, but I fail time and again
For to me it is worth it – Dear Lord, suffer my poor hips
But I'll never ever give up my rissole and chips!

11
OUT AND ABOUT
WITH NATURE

As you may see from this section, I love water, and particularly waterfalls.

I must admit that most of my experience of waterfalls in the valleys is second hand, from pictures posted on social media back home.

I regret not taking the time to enjoy, or even find out about, the many streams and waterfalls that are in the Rhondda.

But I content myself with my imagination, and I think I have a very good one of those! So, I can almost feel the water on my skin and sense the spray, hear the sounds, and I can transport myself there despite not having seen it in "real life".

Valley Stream

My years are now many, and the hiraeth burns
For the Rhondda of my youth I yearn
To walk once again the mountain top,
To breathe clear air, to look, to stop

To find a stream and walk nearby
And watch its hue reflect the sky.
Bubbling, trickling as its voice
Reaches a crescendo, I rejoice.

From small beginnings, I would follow
Occasionally I'll stop and wallow.
Sit awhile and watch it reach
Beloved Rhondda beneath.

As its whisper breaks into a loud call
And it becomes a waterfall,
I'll sit on a rock and dream of days
Gone by, so long ago, no more than a haze.

I know it's only just a dream
But I can almost feel it- my little stream…

Autumn stream

Little stream trickling gently by
What colours you reflect from autumn sky
The richest colours, golds, red and browns
Are now yours to display, your brand - new gown

And dressed in splendour through the woods you dance
To delight anyone who discovers you by chance
Whirling, twirling, flirting with the breeze
That ruffles o'er your water, and through the trees

What secrets have been whispered? Who has kissed
Beside your banks in early morning mists?
You know so much, but you will never tell
But roll on by regardless, through the dell

Bluebells

Where daffodils herald the coming of spring
In a riot of yellow, such cheer do they bring
That other spring flower is much more subdued
And keeps itself a secret, in a dimly lit wood

Tread quietly through, dear reader come hither
And watch the wee bells as they shake, and they quiver
Waving gently from a soft woodland breeze
A carpet of wonder right under the trees

Breathe in the scent of a spring woodland mist
Of a flower that surely by fairies is kissed
Sit among pixies and dream of spring days
Which are gone in a heartbeat with summer's warm haze

So yes, enjoy the daffodil's cheery power
But if peace is desired, seek out another flower
They are here but a moment so walk down to the dell
And celebrate the coming of the magic bluebell

River Rhondda

The Mighty River Rhondda
Both valleys are its source
The Fawr and Fach its parents
The child given life at Porth

In the days when I was young
And when I lived in Rhondda Fach
All my memories were of a river
That was murky, grey and dark

Winding through my little village
Thick and deadened with coal dust
It moved as if it were beaten
But move along it must

Diverted for the pit works
Its natural course was swayed
For the pockets of the wealthy
The Mighty River Rhondda paid

Stripped of all its wildlife
Only the rats remained
The Mighty river Rhondda
Weakened, dying and pained

But as the mining petered
Though the poor had borne the cost
The river started living
As if to say, "All is not lost"

Once the coal dust settled
The fish moved back to stay
Birdlife, and their sweet songs
Are now heard all along the way

Today the wildlife bustles
As the river moves to the ocean floor
The mighty River Rhondda
Is a living being once more

Waterfall 1

See the cold hard rock face

Nothing will move it

But the power of water

Over time will smooth it

See the earth cut

From a glacier long gone

Ice turned to water

And the water rushes on

See the river topple

To the floor from such a height

As a new bride's veil

Gleaming, shining white

See the vapour rise

And froth appear below

As the water gathers

To resume its seaward flow

See the waterfall

Feel its breath against your face

Feel the life within

And the magic in this place

Waterfall 2

Sit a little while
Rest your weary soul
Gaze into the stream
Water pure and cold

Watch it pour on rocks
That glisten round and green
Purifying, clear
Calming, bright and clean

Listen to the sound
Of rapids as they rush
Past each craggy stone
Inspiring artist's brush

Breathe in cool damp air
Stress begins to cease
As the waterfall brings
Overwhelming peace

My Valley, the Mist and Me

Up above where life's troubles are churning
As the cool mist swirls around
I will find an old seat on the hillside
And for a moment I'll rest, looking down

I will hide from a world full of stresses
As on top of the clouds I'm at ease
With only the sound of the crickets
And only the kiss of a breeze

I will smell the sweet scent of the bracken
And I'll watch the red kite soaring high
It's just me and my valley together
The mountain, the mist and the sky…

And really, that is all I need to say about my Valley.

The beauty that was there all along, under the grey of the

pits, is returning once more.

And one day so will I…

Thank you for reading

Julia

ABOUT THE AUTHOR

I was born in 1965 in Llwynypia Hospital into a working class family.
The oldest of three siblings, I lived my early life in Ynyshir

I was encouraged by my Mam to study hard at school and have a career.

In 1988 I qualified as a therapeutic radiographer and have remained in the
same career since.

I currently live in New Zealand with my husband and two grown up
children. I love sewing, and collecting vintage sewing patterns.

Printed in Great Britain
by Amazon

55860533R00080